In Love With
Insanity

by

TERRENCE BULL

Take a journey into Terrence Bull's realm of fantasy and insanity: where a simple urn, forged by a wizard, is destined to fulfil an ancient prophecy; take a glimpse into the world contained inside a single raindrop; discover an army caught in a terrifying faery's dream; see inside the mind of insanity through a tear in the fabric of reality; and discover Adam and Eve's cursed existence; plus many more frightening, entertaining and sometimes hilarious poems and short stories.

In Love With Insanity
by Terrence Bull

ISBN 978-0-463-85996-4

Acknowledgements

This is dedicated to my wife and sons; whose inspiration and encouragement made this book possible and helped me to revive a passion I thought was long gone.

Table of Contents

The Urn

The Maker

A small flame sparked into life as a match was struck across a rough-hewn stone wall. The workroom of the old wizard began to reveal itself as he lit the many half melted candles dotted around the room. The centre piece was a finely inlaid wooden table on which was strewn an array of scrolls, writing implements and oddly shaped devices crafted from wood and various types and hues of metal. The back wall of the chamber was dominated by an enormous stone fireplace. It housed a large cauldron hanging from a cast iron stand, below which was the remnants of yesterday's fire. There were no windows within this chamber as it was buried far beneath a towering castle surrounded by a moat bordering lush green fields that stretched out to the edge of a distant forest beyond which rose snow-capped mountains.

A small knock at the heavy metal banded oaken door opposite the fireplace brought a smile to the wizard's weathered face. He quickly moved to open it and greeted the small girl standing in the passageway struggling under the weight of a large bucket of water.

"Moin!"

The young girl nodded politely to the old man as she shuffled quickly forward to put the bucket down next to the fireplace.

"You are just in time Beatrix. Today we forge the urn Gefäß des Lebens (Vessel of Life)."

This brought a smile to the small girl's face, but she saw in the old man a whisper of sadness behind his resolute smile. Even though she had been waiting eagerly for this day since the tragedy of almost a year ago, she still felt a shiver of fear pass through her.

The Heir

"You cannot simply drag a war horse around by its bit young master!", exclaimed the old teacher to his young charge who was struggling atop a large, powerful and stubborn black stallion. "Use your knees boy! When a sword is in your hand and the battle rages, you won't have want of reins anyway. And, lucky for you, Engel knows it."

9

The boy then let the reins loosen slightly and skilfully guided the horse with the subtle pressure of his knees, turning him from the practice yard into the wide-open fields. He let out a shout as the horse sped off in a graceful, lighting fast, thundering canter towards the towering trees of the distant forest.

The large pitch-black stallion was the king's own treasured war horse. Known by the king's foes as Dunkler Engel (Dark Angel), he was fast and, in the heat of a battle, just as deadly to the king's foes as the fully armoured and trained warrior who rode atop him. Today was the first time that the king's son and heir had been given to ride him. Under the tutelage of the old general, who had also trained the king in his youth, he had quickly subdued the impressive, head strong stallion and was now testing his fearsome speed in an open canter.

Adalbert was a tall, powerful young man. His long dark blonde hair was swept back in the wind: as was his shirt, revealing his finely muscled torso. His strength of character and intelligence shone out of his bright blue eyes as he held the sight of the distant forest in his gaze.

Suddenly he detected a movement amongst the trees. Then the glimmer of steel. In less than a heartbeat an army surged towards him from out of the undergrowth.

Engel reacted even before he could, spinning him around: away from the threat and back towards the safety of the castle. The battle-hardened horse knew his young charge was not armed and that his true master was not on his back. The great horse's speed increased even beyond Adalbert's wildest expectations as they sped away from the charging horde.

As they rode, Adalbert could hear the trumpet sound from the castle's tallest tower, signalling the impending attack. He saw the old general riding out to meet him: carrying in his hand his large double-edged broad sword. The general's fierce look told Adalbert all he needed to know as they both raced back to the castle gates.

He could tell by the colour of their flags that the armoured horsemen thundering up behind them were led by Odoacer, the leader of a brutal Gothic tribe that had been rumoured to have sacked a number of towns far to the south of them. On their long pikes were the heads of the king's scouts, which was why they had had no advanced warning of their approach.

Just a they reached the bridge crossing the moat and were in sight of safety, a heavy arrow slammed into Adalbert's back throwing him forward off his mount. The last thing he saw was the heavy beams of the moat bridge as they raced up to meet him.

The Prophesy

As the wind and rain raged outside, a booming knock echoed throughout the castle. On the king's instruction, the gates where hurriedly opened to a black hooded, wizened old hag clutching a tall staff in her right hand and a large cloth bag in her left. None of the soldiers and king's staff who met her would look into her eyes as they quickly led her to the queen's chamber. As they approached the door, they could hear the cries of the queen in the last throws of labour. To their relief, the old hag waved them away as she threw open the door and strode into the room. The hag quickly shooed away the queen's attendants and then slammed the door shut behind them.

To the nervous attendants waiting just outside the door, it seemed like an eternity before the screams ceased and the cry of a small child was heard. One of them quickly rushed off to summon the king while the rest waited impatiently for the door to be opened to them.

By the time the king had arrived, a crowd had gathered outside the queen's chambers waiting to hear news of the birth. The talking and mummers quickly creased as the king strode up to the door. He turned to those waiting and his stern look sent them scurrying back from the door to a respectful distance. He then took a deep breath and strode inside.

In the arms of the hag was a small child wrapped tightly in cloth. The look on the hag's face said it all. He quickly went to his wife's side as she lay drench in sweat and her own blood. Her face was serene as she looked into her husband's eyes. Just before her life faded completely away, she whispered into his ear.

The king bent forward and kissed his wife on her forehead while choking back his grief. He then slowly stood and went to their child. Taking him into his arms he raised him above his head and proclaimed in a loud voice, "Today, as prophesied by your mother with her dying breath, I say to you my son, and to all who hear, that you are a man of power. Hence fourth you shall be called Adalbert, which is 'noble and bright'. Though evil may befall you, none will conquer your spirit.

Indeed, though your life may be forged in a fragile vessel, it will transcend time and endure forever. Protected by those you love and who love you."

The Urn

Reaching into a golden cage, the wizard gently took two small lizards from inside and brought them across to the cauldron. Whispering an incantation, he thrust his hands and the lizards into the molten liquid. Mere moments later he drew forth a beautiful urn that was shaped with the delicate curves of a women. The lizards had formed into two dragons shaped as handles on each side.

To Beatrix's amazement, as the wizard continued to chant, the story of Adalbert's last ride and death began to form around the sides of the urn. The urn's colour turned to the bronze hue of the boy's tanned skin and the black stallion Engel, with Adalbert riding atop him, reared up in a final salute to his young charge.

While the urn was intricately ornate and the story it told stood out in bold relief, there was not a flaw or maker's mark on it. Nothing about it spoke of the deep secret it held; the soul of the boy it contained and the wonder of its making. It was not what the king had hoped for, a return of his son. None-the-less, it was as the wizard had predicted, and spoken often of, a vessel of life.

It carried the child's prophesy with it and, as the old hag had proclaimed, someday it would find its names sake to pass on the boy's spirit, intelligence, graciousness and strength. It would be possessed by a gentle boy and one day be 'Protected by those you love and who love you.'

Great joy resounded throughout the kingdom when the urn, known as Gefäß des Lebens (Vessel of Life), was presented to the king. All proclaimed that it would herald the return of the king's strength as well as the glory of the kingdom. The king treasured Gefäß des Lebens and placed it inside a glass case beside his throne. Indeed, with it always in his sight, the king did return to his strength and in time restored his kingdom for the sake of his son.

However, as the years became decades and the decades turned into centuries, the story of the urn disappeared into history. Facts became myths and myths turned into legends. Gefäß des Lebens became lost in wars and passed from hand to hand. Eventually it was considered to be but a simple trinket. It crossed continents and oceans and ending up being taken in by a young man who dealt with all manner of history's flotsam and jetsam.

However, there was something about this ornate urn that intrigued him. As he took it from its box and unwrapped it, he swore he saw a flicker of movement in the prancing horse. He heard a faint war cry and felt a chill of fear as if an army of savages pursued him. He was so taken by the urn that he put it into the front window of his small shop. It even took pride of place, ahead of many more illustrious antiques.

As the years passed by, the young man grew older and no one but he saw the treasure in that bronze colour urn. So there it sat, year after year, in its pride of place in his front window, ignored by all.

The Boy

The bell above the door rung as it was hesitantly pushed open by a young boy. He looked around and saw an old man seated quietly at the back of the shop unpacking some old once loved, yet all but forgotten treasures. He quickly glanced in the front window before going up to the old man.

"Excuse me sir. How much is that urn you have in your window?"

The old man was taken aback by the question. In all his years of owning the urn, no one had asked after it. He now felt quite reluctant to part with it.

"What makes you think you could afford such a wonder, young man?"

"Oh! Well I am not sure I can, but I would like to know how much it is so I can save up to buy it. If that is possible?"

This made the old man smile. Here was a boy just as much in love with the old urn as he was. After all these years maybe he could be persuaded to part with it: if the young man proved worthy. So, he gave the boy a price that he knew he couldn't afford to see how he would react. To his surprise, the lad's face grew a smile and he nearly skipped out of the shop promising to return when he had the money.

The first time the boy saw the urn, he swore that the boy's gaze turned to him and the stallion called out a war cry as it rose up even higher on its two back legs. A wind seamed to pass over him, carrying with it the smell of a forest mixed with a tinge of fear.

Every day he passed by, the boy had grown more and more fascinated by the ornate urn in the front window of the old man's shop. One day he plucked up enough courage to go in and ask about it. He was certain that the urn was not for sale as there was no price displayed on it. But now he had its price, he knew that it was only a matter of time until it was his.

The young man came back often to make sure his urn had not sold and eventually he and the old man formed a friendship. Suddenly, out of the blue the old man decided to auction off the urn in a raffle: he said it was a way to promote his business. This both excited and saddened the young man, for while he could afford the price of a ticket, he knew he had little chance of winning the raffle.

As the days went by and the number of tickets being sold increased the boy began to become quite despondent. He knew that the urn would go to some other lucky winner. After all, he had never won anything in his life. When the day of the draw came, he almost refused to go. However, his mother had insisted. So he dragged himself out of bed and made his way into town.

By the time he had arrived at the store, a crowd had gathered, and the old man was standing up to make a speech. Standing at the back of the crowd, the young man did not see that the old man had seen him. After a quick speech, the old man reached into a large hat and drew out a single name. The boy looked down as his eyes almost filled with tears - for he knew he must have lost his precious urn forever.

Then everyone was cheering and slapping him on the back. "Albert, you have won!", they yelled. Thus, with that proclamation, the urn was his!

He was almost scared to hold it the first time for fear of breaking it. It took him weeks to realise that it hadn't all just been a dream and he did indeed own the precious urn.

Something about this ornate urn resonated with him. He felt that it had brought him luck. Along with the urn came a renewed confidence. He almost felt that there was nothing he could not do. Indeed, over time the boy grew into a man and travelled the world. His wits, graciousness and intelligence took him to great heights in many illustrious careers, the urn always with him.

Eventually he discovered the original Germanic form of his name was Adalbert: meaning noble and bright. In honour of the good favour the urn had brought him, he named it Adalbert. When he did so, he saw the boy smile and heard a sigh of joy come from deep within the urn.

The Toy

Dinggly dell, wishing well,
Bibbly bobbly boy.
Precious child's, tame and wild,
coloured knobbly toy.

Clarity of Thought

In a moment stretching beyond reason, a thought reverberates in time.

A drop of water forms in unending slowness. A budding jewel glistening in the sun reflecting a wonder of colour. A small window to another world where all is calm and serene.

Meadows of green undulate under a luminescent turquoise sky. All is silent. A distant eye spies an old thatched cottage planted in a bed of daisies. Tall pines surround their sole charge reaching for the sun. Their toes nuzzle in a vast bed of moss. A small trickle of water carves out its own path. Its laughter runs between giants whose limbs reach across rich banks to hold hands.

White frosting covers towering purple peaks peering over the pine lovers. Ragged grey gems cascade down their slopes, tumbling and cavorting with each other in a game of joyous children.

Melting cold gives birth to laughing brooks, as rivers spring from tears. Rolling, tumbling, fumbling gem children are herded towards a distant shore. Slowly they get lost in a dream and forget themselves. Big angular and bold become small and smooth. Small begets small to birth a myriad of grains. Washed clean they reach the beach and snuggle together in the bright warmth of a friendly sun.

Tiny feet, smooth and soft, dance over the memory of gem children. Each impression is caressed by a crowd of sparkling white fledglings desperate to savour this momentary touch and remember where they came from. Yet soon they are stroked back to sleep and smoothed over by the gentle hand of mother. And such a mother: vast is her reach and powerful her love, filling endless basins to overflowing.

A giggle tinkles over the shore as our child races into her mommy's embrace. Sandy curls skip around light blue eyes full of joy and innocence. Tiny arms circle a tender neck. Rose lips caress rosy checks.

Knowing eyes look to heaven, spying a gathering storm. Whispering soothing blankets of love, mommy whisks her precious away to shelter.

Soon the sky is full to overflowing. Tiny drops fall in unending slowness carrying with them the clarity of thought.

Gast-a-lion

Gast-a-lion from Montpellier,
A talented baker extraordinaire,
Maker of buns one can't compare,
Like Sauvignon and Burnt Eclair,
Angel cakes as light as air,
Tarts so rich we all despair,
The added pounds on our derrière.

A Faery's Dream

A gentle sprinkle of golden dust settled on the ground, sparkling like a million diamonds in the morning sun, and out burst a hound of war: all sharp teeth and deep guttural snarls. Half a dozen men screamed as they collapsed under the huge animal's weight. A shower of blood erupted from the melee along with ruined body parts and sickening cries for help. The stench of human offal mixed with the rancid breath of the monster, making those close to the nightmare gag and turn away: least they lose what little sustenance they had left in their bellies.

Further down the line a hundred men raised a war cry as they dashed forward with their swords raised: charging a wall of waving vines in the last throws of dragging a clutch of men and horses down into the dirt of a beautiful bright green meadow covered in a treasure of daisies and four leaf clover.

A light cool breeze carried the scent of the flowers carpeting the field to those sitting astride their horses on a rise at the back of the army as they directed the fray. That and the twinkle of the first light of dawn betrayed the cruelty of the chaos stretched before them. A frantic gesture from his armour bearer directed General Montgomery's worried gaze to a group of soldiers whose spears had turned into snakes: the steel scales slicing open the delicate flesh of their hands; the bodies of the snakes writhing up their arms; and their huge arrow shaped heads striking out at the hapless men's faces and terrified eyes.

All this horror seemed as a dream: given that their fearsome foe was simply a group of beautiful children, dressed in the lightest of shimmering rainbow coloured lace, dancing and chanting an eerie tune across the moor: all while spreading a fine glittering dust into the wind. Their lovely faces and eyes were contorted in a rapture of concentration as they were caught up in, and totally absorbed by, their deadly ritual.

The faery folk appeared to have no real awareness of the epidemic of fear and death they were laying down with their airily beautiful and hypnotic spells. The very earth rose up in concert with the ephemeral little angels. Almost blindly they frolicked across the daisies and stroked into being gargantuan nightmarish beasts from the very soul of the land: abominations that decimated hundreds of heavily armoured and battle-hardened men and war horses with almost no effort at all.

A tiny speck of dust, drifting over the roar and screams of the combat, found its way to the command post and gently came to rest on the General's cheek.

II

"Montgomery, you look as if you're lost in another of your daydreams."

Suddenly realising he had somehow lost track of time, Professor William Montgomery tried to hide his embarrassment with a gruff reply, "Nonsense, old man, just wondering when this blasted train will get moving again."

"Well, I'm sure there are a lot of people getting on right now that are just as impatient as you are to get to London."

A shrill whistle blew as the train lurched forward and chugged its way out of the station: dragging behind it a billowing black column of soot and dense choking smoke. Montgomery's friend and colleague, Professor Harold Stannard, continued to fill the air with talk of the upcoming day and the frustrations wrought by his 'lazy and stupid' students. He insisted that they all seemed unwilling, or worse, unable to learn even the basics. Montgomery pointed out that most people didn't share Stannard's passion for ancient myths and legends: or the esoteric art of deciphering long lost languages from scrapes of decaying parchment and broken shards of pottery.

He glanced out of the window and was captured by the green of the rolling hills. There was a proliferation of daisies covering the ground: no doubt freshly coaxed up from their winter slumber by the recent warm spring rains. He seemed to be remembering something about the countryside, when Stannard broke into his thoughts with a shout, "Blast! I've spilt this damned tea down my front and now I will look as if I've wet myself: which, no doubt, will be no end of amusement for the riffraff that frequent my lecture hall."

Shocked out of his thoughts of green fields and the smell of daisies, he turned with an annoyed curse trapped just behind his lips and looked his friend in the eye. Just then, as Stannard looked up from hurriedly wiping his lap, Montgomery noticed that there was a strange glint, or maybe some sort of flickering shadow, deep within his friend's eyes. Suddenly the world twisted cruelly about him as he began to fall sideways.

III

His heavy armour helped to drag him off his horse and he landed heavily from 25 hands up. The custom-made breast plate, steel sleeves and leggings proved no protection from the brutal blow that the all too solid ground inflicted on his shoulder and hip. The loud clash of swords, terrified screams of horses and men, and the thunder of warfare broke like a wave over General Montgomery's consciousness. He lay on the ground with the wind knocked out of him and the memories of another man, and a different time, echoing through his mind.

His armour bearer hurriedly scrambled off his horse and struggled to help him to his feet: not knowing that a deep mental disorientation afflicted the General more than the shock and pain of the fall. However, by the time the General was back on his feet, he had recovered his mind and was back in this, the deadliest of battles, ready to command once more.

He quickly surmised that he had been unseated from his horse, and taken into another world, by the magic art of the faeries. He bellowed a command to his fellow officers to move further upwind: away from the threat of their dreaded glistening powder.

On surveying the scene before him, and having himself experienced the power of the enemy, he knew his men didn't stand a chance. They could not fight the faery's spells with steel and physical fortitude alone. So, he immediately ordered a retreat, while unleashing a volley of arrows at the little folk to try and cover his men's backs as they ran for their lives.

Not one of the arrows found their mark. Yet even as ineffective as the arrows were, the mythical creatures still seemed content on maintaining their ground and not advancing on the fleeing soldiers. What is more, once the two armies were separated by 1000 yards, a small group of even younger faeries detached themselves from the main group and strode forward to halfway between the two forces. Assuming it was a delegation of sorts, the General took three of his top officers and rode out to meet them. He reined in his mount with 20 yards still to cover and dismounted: striding the rest of the way on foot with his men in tow.

The youngest of the four faery children stepped forward with a grim look on his face. He captured the general in a mesmerising stare and, while not appearing to speak at all, Montgomery could hear his words clearly in his mind. His voice was like a thousand bells awoken by the blast of a thunderclap and the rushing wind of a hurricane. The General fell to his knees and clasped at his ears in an attempt to block out the din.

His men, horrified at the sight of the General kneeling before them in such pain, drew their swords and made to rush forward. But before they did, a wave of relief washed over Montgomery and he was able to hold up a hand to still his men.

The small faery then spoke with the voice of a man, "We see that your mind cannot contain our language and so we will speak thusly: in sounds that float on the air." His voice was not at all childlike. Yet in its fullness it rung with the clarity and purity of a bell. He spoke in a quiet soft tone, but the very ground vibrated with each word. The officers wondered if it was the wind they heard, or the sound of a distant church bell. Yet the words came out clearly and there was no mistaking that this small entity commanded a great power. He seemed to hold in his hands the very spirit of the earth.

Montgomery, having regained his composure, demanded, "Why did you attack my men?"

The faery simply chimed, "You made to trample across our mother and we simply set our will to stop you from committing such a heinous crime."

"Why did you not warn us first?"

"The very air is our witness and its sweet fragrance an ample warning. The ground is blanketed richly for all to see: a magic carpet that is precious beyond measure. Is it not covered in rarities and charms that even one such as yourself would recognise? To venture forth upon such as this is folly: worthy of no further warning."

"We could see a change in the landscape and its covering, as you say. Yet, we have travelled far and knew not that you possessed this land. Our minds were set on returning home by the shortest path and our supplies could not afford us to take a lengthy detour. We have not encountered such as your kind before in our travels. We have only heard tell of your folk through children's tales and stories told around a campfire: conjured up by those who would seek to strike fear into a gullible listener. We meant no harm. Still, now more than half my men lie dead or dying on the borders of your 'mother'."

The small faery looked deeply into the General's eyes, as if to divine the truth behind his words. He then closed his eyes, as did the three standing behind him: and thus they seemed to communicate with one another. After a moment, the leading faery opened his eyes and sighed, "It seems we have been apart from your kind for far too long. The last encounter we had with you, we were but children and your people had only recently descended from the trees. We took you into our care then, as it seems we must again now: to teach you. Alas, it seems your race has so very short a memory."

And with that he lifted his arms and a great sound came floating on the air from the gathered faeries: both near and far. A veal lifted from the land on which they had fought and there stood Montgomery's men: alive and unharmed. They seemed to all awake, as if from a deep meditation. The scars of war were no longer carved on the ground: as if the battle had never taken place. A fog lifted from the General's mind and he realised that they had merely been trapped in a faery's dream.

IV

Stannard's voice cut through Montgomery's reveries, "So, as I was saying. The ancients always felt that pre-history was dominated by dream states: some real and some imagined. Even the Aboriginals of Australia describe their pre-history as Dreamtime. So, it's not really surprising that we have trouble separating our dreams from reality. I say, are you even listening to me old chap?"

The train shuddering to a halt jolted Montgomery out of his fog and he replied curtly, "What? Yes. Well, dreams are just fine and dandy for those whose lives are spent in myths and legends, but hardly useful for those of us contending with the tangible and rigorous matters of law. Not that some practicing in the courtrooms across our fair land aren't short on making up a story or two when required."

At this quip Stannard laughed, "Too right! And more besides."

Laughing together they both snatched up their briefcases and joined the rest of the crowd jostling for position to get on with their mundane everyday lives.

As Montgomery stepped out of the train's door, something caught his eye. Just for a moment he thought he glimpsed an unusually beautiful child staring at him. Yet, when he turned to look, there was no one there. Momentarily his senses were filled with the scent of daisies and a summer meadow. It was like the strange feeling of déjà vu, but reserved only for his sense of smell.

Before he had time to wonder further about it, everything seemed to suddenly solidify around him. The noise of the station came crashing in like a wave. The pungent odour of smoke and the impenetrable solidity of the sooty grey concrete of the platform coalesced around him and overpowered his confusion.

He noticed that some peculiar dust had speckled the shoulders of his jacket. With an annoyed swipe he dusted himself off then firmly straightened his bowler hat. With a proud determination, he shrugged off this daydreaming nonsense and set off after Stannard: whose back he could just see disappearing into the crowd.

The Old Stump

An old gnarled stump sits alone in darkness remembering its youth, drowning in self-pity.

Hope left him alone eons ago and was quickly replaced with a gnawing hatred. "It's all their fault!", churns around in his mind over and over again. "I did all I could.", is the lie that feeds his deception. The hole where Love should live has slowly filled with anger and malice.

Addictions of lust swim endlessly around his mind - tormenting and demanding constant attention. Each time he gives in, he is relieved and yet filled to the brim with self-hatred. Your knowing torments him. He needs you and yet wants you gone so your recriminations will no longer taint his lust with the knowledge of sin.

The seedlings moved on an eternity ago. Yet their cries are still fresh in his ears. He closes his eyes and craves the darkness of the deep forest, but reminders crash in on his solitude when they are least expected. Just as his conscience is falling asleep, it is jarred awake by the sorrowful moans of the inflicted. Hurts are pounded home by demands of justice.

Each attack just strengthens his unforgiving bark. The scars have coalesced to form an impenetrable armour. The slings and arrows of righteousness simply skip away unhindered in their dance. The itch of wounded souls has all but ceased.

Yet his anger flares when a barb breaks into his dead lies.

Penetrating and drawing tears of sap from the last reserves that have all but turned to dust. The fury is a cloak worn to scare those who would waken his remorse and explode deeply buried charges of guilt. The ancient stump then raises his powerful branches and fails about in rage. A dark wind rushes over the rotting earth beneath his feet and kicks up all manner of dead remnants of life and growth. He stamps his feet seeking to crush out the life that has dared to intrude on his death watch.

But soon your voice is there to smooth the way again with lies and comforting deceptions. To stroke away the awakening. To bring back the comfort of darkness and a deep solitude. "It's you against the world, my love.", you croon softly. Your words are a velvety fragrant oil that covers over the vile muck: soothing the old stump back to sleep and to dreams of a quiet guiltless death. For what more can we hope for?

Hatred is a comfort, a balm that cries, "No one understands!" It keeps away the touches of light that would expose you. It pours out the oil of sleep. Yet there is no rest, just all-consuming harried hatred.

Sit alone my old stump and fade to death surrounded by the rot of hollow lies and insincere promises. What more could you hope for?

The Stare

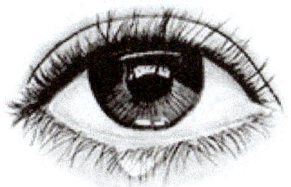

Turquoise lace floats in a clear white globe tinged by small dark feathers. A soul peers from inside: a deep well of life and understanding.

Beyond a cheeky gleam, a spark of truth peeks out: a knowing that tells a tale and shines with a promise and a warning. Delight bubbles softly beneath a quiet pool of awe. Questions are being asked in a soundless stare. Expectations are being measured and resolve is being prodded and tested. "How far will you go?", is being asked.

Deeper still is a sadness. A joy lost: a wish unfulfilled. Buried far beneath the sensual smile is a river of loss. A want is left wanting: a love is left longing. It calls for satisfaction and for its fire to be quenched. Maybe a small tear is the river overflowing and seeking to drown the self-flagellation.

But then that shutter is closed and, along with a sigh, a stern resolve comes barking forth. An open challenge: "Can you truly care or have you no more depth than your lust?" Your ire rises to meet the challenge, even though you want to shy away. You tunnel even deeper seeking the real treasure hidden to everyone but the blessed few.

And you are not left unrewarded. The heart of this soul breaks forth in a blinding blaze of rich colours and astonishing surprises. "There be gold here!", your heart cries out. "How has no one discovered this cave of treasures before?", shouts out from your eyes.

A hand reaches across the divide. Smooth satin moulds around soft curves of wonder.

A lightning bolt strikes and the shock throws you both away back into your now. With the echo of wonderment reverberating in your dreams.

Fantail

Your love is like a Fantail. Flitting around my head just out of reach. Your petite beauty and flirting, darting mystery enraptures me and captures me.

Just knowing you are with me comforts me in the dark forest. Your chittering keeps me company and tells me I am not alone. The steel hard Rimu is aloof in its majesty. The Kauri's warm arms are unreachable as they cradle and guard the favoured few. The Pepper Tree's five fingered leaves provide spice, but no lasting comfort. The Ferns and Ponga Trees with their Koru promise an exotic life. Yet to touch them is sharp and rough. None of these, your silent cousins, can comfort me as you do my tiny love. Only in their destruction can they be used by me.

But why destroy such ancient wonders? Their cold presence may keep me in the dark, but they are your home. This is where you dwell. This dark glade of beauty and timelessness, a habitat both of wonder and strangeness, is your native land. And even if I am only permitted for a small time to enter your world. Gladly I would endure their hard stares and rough barks of impenetrable exclusion to spend time with you my Fantail.

I long to hold you and make you mine, but I know this would corrupt what you are. A tame Fantail would no longer be a Fantail. It would be a sad parody. A stuffed toy in the cruel hands of a child. Dragged from room to room as they search out new pleasures. Your presence being enough; your inactive participation sufficient to calm their tantrums.

Once you alighted on my shoulder. You even sat in my hand and took the gifts I offered. Your touch was exquisite. It electrified and thrilled me. For a moment I had hope. I imagined a world with you always with me. Us forever together. But then you danced away again. Tantalisingly close. A tiny star of light flickering around my head. An act of God that changed me forever. Freeing me yet binding and taunting me to the knowledge of my ungainly difference.

My feet tread in the dirt. I cannot fly like you my Fantail. You dart to and fro; I stamp along, slogging to keep up. You stay with me, yet constantly flit ahead. Are you showing me the way, or showing me how slow and awkward I am?

I know you think my love is not real. The song of the Tui may sometimes entice me, I may even glance as a Kererū thunders by, but my constant delight is in you my Fantail. No other could ever take your place in my heart.

I am not so stupid that I do not know that this journey must end. I will reach a clearing and you will dart out to me then retreat back into the delights of your world. We will regard each other across the chasm of inches as I move further away to the light and you remain in the comforting arms of giants.

But for now, stay with me my little wonder. Let me know you are near. For you are my only comfort in this strange world. You make the shadows bearable and the journey through the forest light. I would skip along to show you my joy if I was not so tired and my boots so heavy.

Come inside my Bivouac. It is warm in here. Do not fear that I will trap you. For your beauty is in your freedom and I am sworn to keep you free. I will keep my lusts in check as I watch your tantalising dance. Know that you are in control and I am your willing slave.

Just let me be with you my Fantail. Let me dream for a little longer that you are mine.

The Profit

I see too much

It all started on that day. Colours were just more vivid. Everything stood out in stark 3D - as if previously I had only been seeing the world in 2D. Motives became obvious; as did lies. I could see through every subtle misdirection and attempt to beguile and mislead.

More than this, I could easily see the future. Not in a spooky way. It was simply an obvious deduction based on the current set of circumstances: a pulling together of seemingly random disconnected pieces of information into, for me, a predictable conclusion.

I say too much

You started telling me to be careful of what I say. You told me that your Mother often told you that our words are powerful. She explained that they can change the future and you were worried that maybe my predictions are not just a foretelling, but somehow shaping the outcome. Yet, at the time I thought I knew better: I was simply telling it like I saw it.

Then everything changed

The changes were only subtle to begin with: a lessening of our financial stability and the small decline in your health. But they all added to a slow decent into hopelessness.

In the beginning, when I still had hope, I managed to keep my faith and to let go to a higher will. I could believe that everything would be ok as long as I simply trusted that there was a plan: a plan for good. One that would bring us no harm and give us hope. A plan that would mean it would all be ok in the end. A plan that would even bring us prosperity!

Yet everything just got worse. The slow decline became a free fall towards an eventual destruction. I just couldn't trust anymore. I really tried: doing everything prescribed - and more. But we kept getting poorer and you kept getting sicker. My hope was gone.

As I was writing my latest post, a foretelling based on the obvious truth surrounding us, a small thought snuck in: 'Don't just say what you see, say what you want to see', it whispered.

To be honest, it scared me. I knew it was wrong. I would be playing with fate. I would be going from being a scribe to taking on the role of the creator. A power I neither wanted to assume nor wished to wield.

There were so many warnings about this from the past. Every scholar had written of this danger. No one had ever succeeded in assuming this role and come out ahead. Every myth and legend portrayed this tale: a rise to power; an unnatural desire to take more power; an unholy alliance that led to the seizing of unimaginable power; then the inevitable fall to destruction. All those seeking this omnipotence were labelled fools.

But you were dying. What else could I do? I no longer had the faith to trust.

So I wrote just a little more than I saw. I added my own outcome. Yet worse than this, I signed it as being a word of truth - not a word of hope.

After all, I could have just said, 'Wouldn't it be nice if...?' And what would have been wrong with that? But no, I had to go that step too far and proclaim my own will as a word of fact.

I ignored the warnings and went ahead anyway. How could I have predicted this would happen? Oh, I knew there would be consequences, but not this!

Now I've said too much

I need you to know that I don't write my posts anymore. I don't tell of what I see and what is to come. I have learnt my lesson. This power is too great for me.

You are my ever-present rebuke. A punishment I will never be done with.

Your life is an obvious lie. A lie I fabricated

Though you walk around, everyone can see you are no longer alive. I cannot hide my guilt any longer. Your skin is rotting away and falls from your bones. You have the stench of the grave always about you and your beautiful eyes and rich hair have all but turned to white. Your vacant shambling and constant groaning are cries of a soul trapped in constant agony and decay with no hope of release. I have trapped you, my love, in an eternal torture. My only hope now is for fire to be your freedom and my absolution.

I have covered us both with petrol and the lighter is in my hand. May we both be granted peace in this, my final prophecy.

This, my final word

Welcome Gnome

Gliding across a luscious carpet of vibrant green and delicate baby tears, my awareness settles on your sky-blue britches buried knee deep in the lush overgrowth. Your grass green tunic, held tightly around your plump middle by a wide black belt with a strong golden buckle, reflects and matches the colour of the baby tears as it wraps you in its warm arms. The lamp you hold, while having never been lit, shines the way for all those who enter. A welcome sign under an old gentle tree, waving a friendly hello, just off a well-trodden, old fashioned, red brick path. Your age-old smile, buried in a long white beard, is reflected in your wise, dark eyes. Even though you have never seen me, I can feel your greeting and acceptance as I pass you by.

I wonder how long you have lived there under that tree. How patient you must be: when the weather is cold and the wind blows leaves in your face; when the laughter of children pass you by without even a glance or a loving stare; when your family is too busy with the shopping to give you a friendly 'Hi there!'. Does the rain provide your tears when your eyes have run dry? Does the wind sing to you and sooth you to sleep? Do the birds greet you at the start of each new day? Or are you simply alone and unnoticed? A simple ornament, and nothing more, to those who stranded you there under the arms of your mother, the kind old gnarled friendly giant.

I long to take you in my arms and bring you indoors. Where it's warm and sheltered from the rain and the storms. Where there's always the sounds of a family in love and the purr of a cat and the fun of a dog as it plays for a hug. Could it be that you've heard them, outside under your mother, the tree? Have you longed to be with them and see what I see? Or are you content and I'm simply making a fuss. When all that you wish for is to stare at each sunset and contemplate the shadows as they disappear in the morning and appear again at the end of the day, fading to grey at the last light of dusk.

Do you know you have friends? One under a mushroom and a one on top of a house: one reading a book; one lying down, quiet as a mouse. All three of you sit out each day, not giving yourselves away. But do you get together at night? Do you meet in the darkness, when we're all asleep? Do you greet in the old ways, with a handshake or a nod? Are there ancient rituals you perform, when we cannot hear you? Do you summon up songs that tell of your travels or tell each other the news that you heard whispered on the wind? The stories of your cousins and uncles and brothers that drift in from all over the world. Bathing in the wonders the others have seen as they sit there and contemplate long days buried in green.

As Easy As

I saw the danger, it was plain to see.
A slimy log, greased in green.
But it was the only way to cross the stream.
With care and balance I could make it work.

Slow and steady, that's the trick.
Step one was not so bad.
A little dodgy, but I made it stick.

I rubbed a little, scrubbed away the moss.
It coloured my shoes, but no great loss.
I just had to concentrate to get across.

Besides, you'd already made it there.
Calling to me with a wicked smile.
I know now what you did:
your smile growing as I slid.

I stumbled on: step two and three,
as you beckoned me;
step three and four,
just one step more.

But then my knee went out, it took a turn.
I heard it pop, but I didn't stop.
I tried to hop: my one last hope,
as I reached out to grab the rope.

Then I saw your face and I knew it was over.
You went quite calm as you looked down
 at the twine wrapped around your palm.

My only hope was dragged away.
I could see it now, you never intended to stay.

Our love was over yesterday.
This walk in the park was just your way
to lead me astray.

You always meant to leave today.

As once I'd fallen for you,
hopelessly in love, now I was in a stew.
Standing here with nothing left to do,
except finish the job:
surrender to gravity; just give in;
accept the end was here.

In the end,
letting go of you was not a slog.
It was as easy as
falling off a log.

Bad Language

The seagulls holding hands sought refuge in the lush fields of dew-covered shingles.

It is no longer safe out here in the wilderness of plain speak and free thought. I long to protect you from confusion and sprinkle your dreams with the obvious. I want to teach you the patterns of honesty such as I was filled with in my youth. But your world is different, and you are already a child of the bent reality prescribed by norms.

Too late for you, too late for me. To want to be uncompromised is folly. To live, to die with understanding and knowing is too much. Too late my seagull. Perch upon your shingles and sip the dew. Drink in the lies and find comfort in your causes.

I say I will and yet they hear I won't. I plead forgiveness; and it is an admission of intent to harm. I promise no certainty of outcome; now this is a binding contract giving an undeniable bounty of riches. I say hard work; they hear easy. I say time consuming; they hear instant. In all this, I am to blame and must be punished.

In a world turned upside down, heaven is hell; and hell is to be sort after at any cost. Beauty is shunned for deformity. What is pure is perverted.

Of course, you are right, and I am wrong. How else can I withstand the tidal wave of the illogical and survive? My mind needs your re-education. Lock me away in your institutions of septic rightness. My disease must be eradicated from this earth and washed away with passionate rhetoric. The boils which fester in my mouth need lancing and my bile cleansed of reason. Teach me little seagull.

Dare not the word insanity pass my lips, for such an insult would enrage and detonate an already ticking bomb. As my finger points, so three others return the blame: accusing the pointer of the crime being pointed at. My log is too great a burden for me, give me your speck of dust instead. Hold my eyes open and fill them with your dust, then there will be no more room for the forest that blinds me.

You are beautiful. Have I told you this before, seagull? Your ink flows over your body as oil over a white sheet. Metal breaks your smooth lines and sharpens any softness. Dark rims your eyes to drag in any remaining light. A cascade of spiky colours flow over your shaven crown speaking of a lingering promise of joy removed. Every untamed bulge and distorted feature is magnified by your carefully selected uniform. No opportunity to shock has been missed. You are a statue of indignity and unloveliness. You must be so proud.

Fly high my seagull and cook the sun with your radiant iron wings. Extinguish any warmth and light that threatens your darkness. Let's live inside the soil and bask in its solitude. Dig down to the cold interior and freeze the earth. Heat is to be shunned; light is a burden to be eradicated. All my dimly lit halls reveal too much. Obliterate the remaining light and let us bask in the darkness forever.

The storms rage across your brows. Every small disturbance is reflected in your eyes. Your waving hands gesticulate for lost causes and broken promises. Blackened lips pout and stretch wide to let forth your screeching woes.

We are all guilty, none is pure. Yours and my conscience are no longer clean. We bath in mud and swig from rotten mugs overflowing with the vile froth of displeasure. Our sweet tooth has decayed and fallen from our crying mouths. A long goodbye is all we can sustain or endure.

Has my uttering disturbed you? Think not on what I say, it is merely the rantings of a fool who can no longer hold his tongue. Think instead on this world and its beauty. It is a fascination to fly over. Skim across its surface and behold its dewy shingles. There is still a lushness you will perceive, a richness you will discover. Open your eyes, if you can, and drink in the waters of wonder.

I am old, my tiny seagull. I have grown apart from the earth and no longer am bound by its rules. You see me as an abomination, and so it may be, but I have different eyes than you. You may say my sight is clouded, but I have a clarity you cannot understand.

Fear not, for when I am gone from you, I will be no more, and my thoughts and logic will no longer disturb you. You can wrap a blanket of comforting confusion around your shoulders and imagine me to be just a dream. You can bask in illusion and hide behind a solid wall of wailing. You can abide where echoes reverberate, and no one can tell you that you are wrong. You can make up new words, soil and twist the old ones around to suit your needs and shout their reality into being. You can moralise and condemn my bad language to the annuals of history where it belongs.

The seagulls scream as they wheel around an old bloated forgotten corpse.

The Tear

When the tear appeared, an ugly cut slashed across our peaceful realty, we knew it could never be closed and we could never come back from what we had seen: what had been indelibly painted on our eyes and etched on our minds. Stark ugly colours depicting a scene of horror. Already our brains were screaming for relief. They had overloaded with bright contrasts. Hues and patterns crashed upon the shores of our simplicity: the beauty of nothingness that had wrapped us in its warm blanket of sameness since time began—our world of cushioned white and nothing more.

Oh, what terror was stabbed deep into our flesh: striking at our beating hearts. Long knives of existence slicing at the very fabric of our world. Sharpened steel flowing molten into our veins: reaching the tip of every extremity. Unrelenting conveyors of pain soaking into the fabric of our very being.

Now I could even describe the horror. The burst of sounds and smells and words that flowed into our bland and beautiful eternity crashed in and brought with them understanding. We could no longer bath in unknowing. The serenity of unawareness was no longer covering us. We could no longer hide in our vacuum. Instead we now knew, saints forgive us, we knew and understood what had happened; what we had done. The fullness of our guilt plunged stinking talons deep into our overly excited flesh.

Your warm embrace, my love, was unbuckled from around us. Your tight hug encircling us was taken away. The warmth of your flesh that had surrounded us was no more our ever-present comfort. Oh, it's true, we had struggled against your arms and rejected your grip in that long-lost beginning, but over the years you had become our only hope: our sanctuary from the dread of just floating away into the void. Yet, far from the void taking us, it has invaded our world and has become who we are. Until this tear appeared, this portal to another world and another existence.

We tried scratching out our eyes to remove the offence of colour from our seared brains, but to no avail. The intruders stopped us from gaining even this merger relief. Some of us simply blinked out of existence: the knowing revealing the lie that kept them alive. Some babbled, some cried, but most cloaked themselves in a cunning silence: hoping that they would not be noticed and thus left to fester unharmed.

The stench of flesh, the fetor of food, the malodorous reek of warmth from the corridor beyond ate its ugly way up our nose and into our delicate senses. Excruciating sounds of gentle succouring mews thrust inside our ears and pierced our mind. How could this reality come crashing in now after we had finally achieved the blankness of the unknowing, unloving, empty, yet empathetic void? So cruel a turn of fate!

We had no voice: our betraying vocal cords had been ripped out and bloodied by our collective incessant screams. The metallic taste of blood filled our throats and sustained us as we fell into our dreams. We had all pulled out their gossamer fine cables that they had implanted all over our skulls: denying them the chance to listen into our thoughts. All they could see was the cold light shining from our eyes: betraying our every thought. But we could no longer close our eyes as the flaps that covered them were pinned back by the blood from the wires we tore from our heads.

Even in their stupidity, they seemed to perceive our pain from being exposed to their world. They closed the door behind them, in a vain attempt to seal the tear in our world. Alas, but it was all too late. The filth of their existence had already been thrust into our consciousness and we could no longer ignore it and return to the void.

What is worse, our guilt was now fully formed and before us for all to see.

"Which of his personalities do you think is in control now, Doctor?"

"Who can tell? There are just so many of them now. Let's just clean him up and see if we can make him a bit more presentable for his family."

Onion Pie

I love you like an onion pie
Your beauty gets in my eye
And makes me want to cry and cry
I love you, beautiful onion pie

There's layers there below the crust
Deeper down I go, I must
Reach your heart and gain your trust
Below my crust, I gain your trust

Sweet and savory is your heart
The spice of life, yet just the start
My onion pie is not a tart
A meal to fill, one so smart

Joy

A spark of joy explodes over my wilted psyche—a rumble of expectation bringing hope. A small sliver of a smile extends my lips and indents my cheeks. My eyes are squint with pleasure—growing lines of laughter that reach towards my ears. A quiet chuckle murmurs out of my throat and erupts past my grinning teeth. It is a mystery of bliss.

Endorphins flood my brain... but this description is too clinical for the pleasure I feel. Rather, I am filled to overflowing with a sense of peace and love—and there you are. It is you—it always has been.

You are my sunshine, my all, my joy, my pleasure, my peace, my harmony in a troubled world. I never settled—no! I achieved greatness when you said yes. All can see. What is more, all have seen. Your love covers me with a cloak of pride and a shine of beauty. Joy is your name.

We have built foundations, you and I. Children, a gift to this world, and a home for them and us to always return to. An oasis of grass and nature surrounding warmth and comfort. Wrapping them and us in safety and security. No trouble shall cross its threshold.

But why speak of trouble? There is none, but what our imaginations conjure. The future is rosy and bright. A light to shine out into the ages to come. A beacon of hope and a torch of content. Let not our daily ripples cause waves. They are but a soothing word away from calm.

Instead, wrap yourself in my arms and drift away on my dreams. For joy you are to me and joy I can be to you also. Full of life and love. Complete.

Short Story

I like telling stories. Any type really, but short stories are best. They are simple and easy to tell; take little time; and usually have a nice twist at the end. However, it is not often one finds oneself in a short story. Yet today, it happened to me.

I can't say that the day started differently. There was no red moon or orange sky to herald in the sun. Nothing out of the ordinary that signalled that today would be the day I lived a fantasy. The day that everything changed—well at least for me.

If I think hard about the circumstances of my waking moments, I can tell that something was not right. But who thinks that hard in the morning? One simply gets up from their bed, trying not to make too much noise, and gets on with one's usual morning routine. Not much in the way of thought goes into it. So, this morning, when I awoke, I walked into the day as a blind man walks into a wall: completely oblivious that there would be something profound about to happen.

Of course, with the twenty-twenty vision of hindsight, it is quite obvious really. Most would say I was a fool to have missed the signs. But how many have walked in my shoes? How many wake up on an everyday day expecting a miracle? Not me! Yes, it is true to say that my dreams should have given the game away—but, to me, they were just that: dreams. Mere fanciful illusions of a delirious mind in the throes of struggling to the surface of a night drenched in darkness and sleep. If you were me, would you have believed such dreams and woken prepared for what was to come?

Sorry! That's not really a fair question, is it? You don't know what happened, do you? As I haven't told you yet, have I? Do you sense that I am delaying the telling of my tale? I am teetering here on the brink of a cliff. Knowing that going over its edge and falling into its gapping mouth will mean that all that could have been a dream will become real. It will grow flesh and solidify into a living being that I can never be rid of. My short story will no longer be a fairy tale told to children as they prepare for sleep, but a concrete edifice standing stark against the sky proclaiming the truth. There will be no going back. My short story will be complete.

Now that I have lived through from beginning to end, and seen its form in its entirety, I can tell you how it began. It started in a dream. In a wash of emotions dragging me up from a peaceful slumber. No wonder I awoke and simply wanted to start my day in the usual way—as an escape from my night terrors.

Not that I am used to having nightmares, you understand. It just seemed that getting up and on with my day, with the ordinary of the everyday, I would be free of the dream and be able to put it behind me. Instead, I stepped from the hauntings of my mind into the night's shadows—and they became real.

I make it sound like a horror story, but is it really? Maybe to some, but for me? Well, I am still trying to decide what it truly means for me. Maybe, this story will be just another chapter in my life and leave but a remnant of its passing in my psyche—too small to make any appreciable difference to my character. Or maybe this short story will forever define me. Will I even know whether it has changed me or simply defined what is already a part of me? Perhaps you can decide and tell me what you think. But first I must tell you the tale in order for you to understand—in order for you to gain the insight needed to perceive any change.

Many say I am not your standard run-of-the-mill person anyway. Some call me mad: others, a genius. I am outgoing, but socially awkward. My somewhat handsome looks get me further than my social skills can. I never play by the rules—which always gets me into trouble. I both want other's approval, and care not what others think. I will invariably speak when I should shut-up—and I always say way too much. I like to be alone but need the constant company of others to stop from dwelling on my faults and going insane. I preen because I care but wonder who I care about. The dichotomy of my nature drives many to despair and others to over care. I find that, in reality, I comfortably fit nowhere.

So now you know me, maybe you can decipher what comes next.

The wind whistled through the trees outside my window. Its breath was cold and carried the smell of ice and snow upon it. The constant hum of the heat pump had long ago ceased as it lost its fight against the chill. Frozen air seeped up from the floor and turned the condensation on the windows to ice. The winter bed covers were my only protection from the arctic wind, but even they were too thin to resist its deathly grip. My dreams were of fire as my blood turned to ice.

I crawled from our bed, trying to be quiet as I stamped life into my feet. The floorboards creaked as I creeped from the room—you were still asleep. The hallway's sheep skin rugs seemed as flurries of snow upon the cruel ground—I avoided their heat as I stole from our room—still dazed and confused by my dreams.

It was still night, but I could see beyond the darkness as I made my way through the house. The bathroom light exploded in my eyes when I flicked on the switch. I cowered from its warmth, still dreaming of cold. Maybe, I thought, the shower would warm me up. But the water trickling from the head simply refused to show any signs of heating up. It mocked my curses and eventually petered out—becoming but a drip, well suited for nothing but torture.

My delirium deepened as I stumbled from room-to-room determined to escape the cold. Yet it chased me wherever I went and seemed to simply penetrate deeper into my bones. My breath had long ago frozen, so even the steam was gone. I could only blow more cold into my cupped hands. I wrapped myself in one of your crocheted rugs— then I thought of you, my love.

And my horror awoke.

Had I seen you move? Had I heard your breathing?

I rushed to our room and touched your face. It was like icy porcelain—hard and cold and flawlessly smooth. Your eyes were closed, but I knew that they were but white lifeless jelly—staring down the endless tunnel of eternity. Your lips were a pale dead blue. All your kisses were gone. They had escaped with you—stolen away by the cold of this night.

The news had warned of the change to come. But we were secure in our modern home. What could touch us? We had the internet and computers and every modern convenience. We had become comfortable and careless. Another cold snap could not harm us—could it? It was merely another night weathering a southerly chill, we told ourselves.

Yet, this was no southerly. The sun had died and there would be no more warmth—we were told. But who believes these fear-mongers? Who trusts these so-called scientists: who gather millions in funding by spinning a woeful tale? Lining their pockets with our taxes as we work our fingers to the bone yet starve for lack of money. They debate and collude with our leaders to grab for our cash—not caring that we must eat to survive.

What difference did they make anyway? The sun still went out and not even a handful could escape—be it to the warmth of our core or the promise of a new sun ten lifetimes away. Their promises of rescue meant nothing to us. For we did not live in Washington or New York or London or Paris. We lived at the far ends of the earth in a small paradise. Far from the noise and the panic—but not far enough to escape their fate.

We had determined to simply carry on. To plan for our future and to not look back. To hoped that the fears were not real. What else could we do? We were not the rich—with their spaceships and drills. We could not sail away in the dying solar winds or hide in shafts made of steel and concrete—powered by a nuclear fuel that would last a thousand lifetimes. We were just ordinary slobs in an ordinary world—no matter what we hoped.

But is this the end of my short story? Is this how the tale concludes? With me a frozen ghost haunting my home and my love gone. With the end of the world and the dying of the light. Is this all there is?

In the beginning I promised a twist—and here it is, my friend.

When a sun dies, it goes out with a bang. And ours was no different. All the rich were incinerated in their carefully laid plans. The spaceships and tunnels were turned to superheated dust as the shock wave of our exploding star overtook them. Did they really think they could escape?

We knew better and lived our last days in joy. So, when the end came and I awoke from my dreams of cold, you were there to greet me. Your open arms were wide, and I fell into your loving embrace. We were at peace after all. Nothing more could touch us. We had all of eternity to celebrate and share with our loved ones. So, the earth, and indeed our whole solar system was gone, but not our future. For everyone's future— or at least those who plan ahead and understand the truth—is settled in eternity: for those who find peace.

A Shadow in the Night

I can show you the sights
That'll take you to heights
I can show you it right
I can show you, I can show you

Have you seen what's right?
Have you seen this night?
It's out of sight
Can you see it, can you see it?

It's only the wind blowing over the rim
Just a hollow moon. Yes, you'll see it soon

It takes all night, but there's no one like
The olden days when he starts to say

It's a shadow in the night
It's white on white
It's green on green
A shadow in the night
Have you seen it, have you seen it?

If you look just right
If you hold on tight
You can spy it right
A shadow in the night
Have you seen him, have you seen him?

It's over the moon
It'll make you swoon
I've stop too soon

I Remember It All

I was there in the beginning—so were you. It's just that you can't remember. That's the difference between you and me, I remember—everything. I wish I was like you. I wish I could also forget what we did.

I know it's silly to ask, but can you remember the taste of the apple? It was so sweet. Juicy and succulent. I didn't regret eating it. I knew it wasn't an apple—even though you swore it was. The snake wasn't a snake either. He was beautiful. He shone like a star but had such sad eyes. I knew you had talked to him. That was your first mistake. He said, 'Don't talk to the him—he's a snake.' I know that he told you this, because I remember everything.

Why wouldn't I eat the fruit? I loved you so much. You were so young then—so innocent. You had gone beyond me by taking that bite and I didn't want to lose you. I could see the change in your eyes. You thought you could see everything more clearly, but your light was already fading. You had passed beyond the veil and were drifting away. I knew that the only way I could stay with you was to join you in the darkness.

I know you can't remember but taking that first bite really hurt. The pain of leaving the light and falling into the world—with its hardness and sharp physical reality—was so severe. I still remember the flash of searing heat as my spirit was rendered from my body. But what hurt the most was the agony of remembering—and knowing that you didn't.

I knew what we had lost. I remembered the joy. The loss of paradise was real for me, but for you it was just another day to survive in the world. You didn't know any better. And why should you have? He made you for me. You were mine to protect and I let you down.

I could have commanded the snake to leave, but he had such sad eyes. He had already lost his glory and his exulted position to us—to me. He had been made subject to my will and I took pity on him. After all, what did I know? I was just a child like you.

But that was then. We are old now—as old as the hills. We have seen mountains come and go, oceans flood and recede. We have witnessed the coming of the ice and the dying of giants. We have watched as our children have grown into nations and spread throughout the earth. We have seen them forget that they are brothers and turn to war—scrapping over land and resources when there is abundance for all.

I stopped trying to help. When I left the council after 900 years of struggling with them, they had a celebration as they buried any memory of me. For them I passed away—no longer a thorn in their side and a voice of reason to dissuade them from their evil thoughts. But the snake, he remembers also—and his eyes are no longer sad.

He is still there whispering in their ears. Of course, they can't see him. They think his ideas are their own. You know I tried to stop him, but what authority do I have now? When I took that bite and was thrown down, I became no better than him. He and I became one—two sides of the same coin. Fate flipped us and I fell with my face in the dirt.

Forgive my ramblings my love. I know you think me an old fool—with my stories and tales of woe. You think you are still young—still in your 40's. As I take you throughout the world, changing cities every 20 years or so, you still believe you are mortal, and you dream of the wonders of growing old together.

How many lives have we lived now? Too many for me to count. I have worked the land and set my hand to every craft and profession known. It has been centuries since we last needed money. You think we are gentry—and sometimes I let you revel in our fame and fortune. Yet, most of the time we are only one step away from being discovered and I must constantly reinvent our lives.

Noah knew not of us—even though we were on his boat. For God hid us from him. We have been gods in Egypt and kings in Europe, settlers of the new world and explorers. Yet, through all of this I have never known peace—for I remember who we are and what we did.

Now as you sleep, I once again tell you our story—for even the quiet of sleep is denied me. In the morning you will awake and believe whatever I tell you. For you, all will be well, and it will simply be yet another day. But not for me. For I remember. I remember it all.

Invite Me In

Invite me into your dark room
Where horror and love live together as one
Where pain and sorrow create a beautiful melody
Where I can be myself without shame

Call me into the light
I want to see the glow of your eyes
I want to know the peace of your love
I want to know all of you without shame

Seek me out
When I'm lost and alone
When I have forgotten who I am
When I no longer know my name
Only my shame

About the Author

Terrence Bull was born in his mom's and dad's bed on a farm in Hawkes Bay, New Zealand in the 1960s. Having to overcome dyslexia, he didn't read his first full book until he was 13 years old—it was 'The Hobbit' by J.R.R. Tolkien. He then read the whole 'Lord of the Rings' trilogy that summer, and by the end had caught the reader's fever.

One of his first lyrical prose stories, in his first year of secondary school, scored him an 'F' and almost got him caned—as his English teacher decided that he must have plagiarized it. He didn't begin any serious fiction writing again until his wife and son encouraged him to give it a go and show them what he could do—that was in 2016.

He wrote 'Bad Language', which shocked and surprised them. He then wrote 'Clarity of Thought' and with their encouragement began writing this book of short stories, poems and lyrical prose.

He now has many more written works that are underway as he begins to take a cautious step into the world of writing fiction.

Connect with Terrence Bull

I really appreciate you reading my book!

For extra bonus material, if you want to contact me, find out more about this book or get a comprehensive link tree to all my socials, go to:

www.inlovewithinsanity.woo.co

www.ingramcontent.com/pod-product-compliance
Lightning Source LLC
Chambersburg PA
CBHW060336260626
47160CB00007B/2810